A Box of Socks

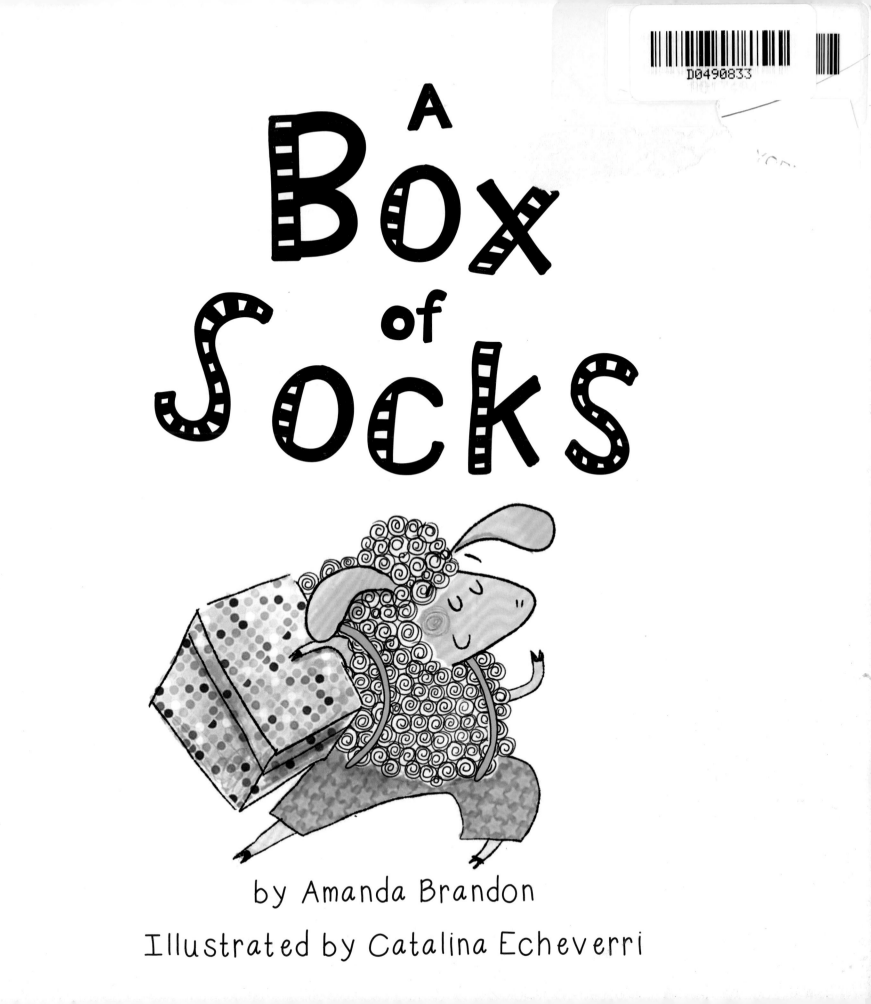

by Amanda Brandon

Illustrated by Catalina Echeverri

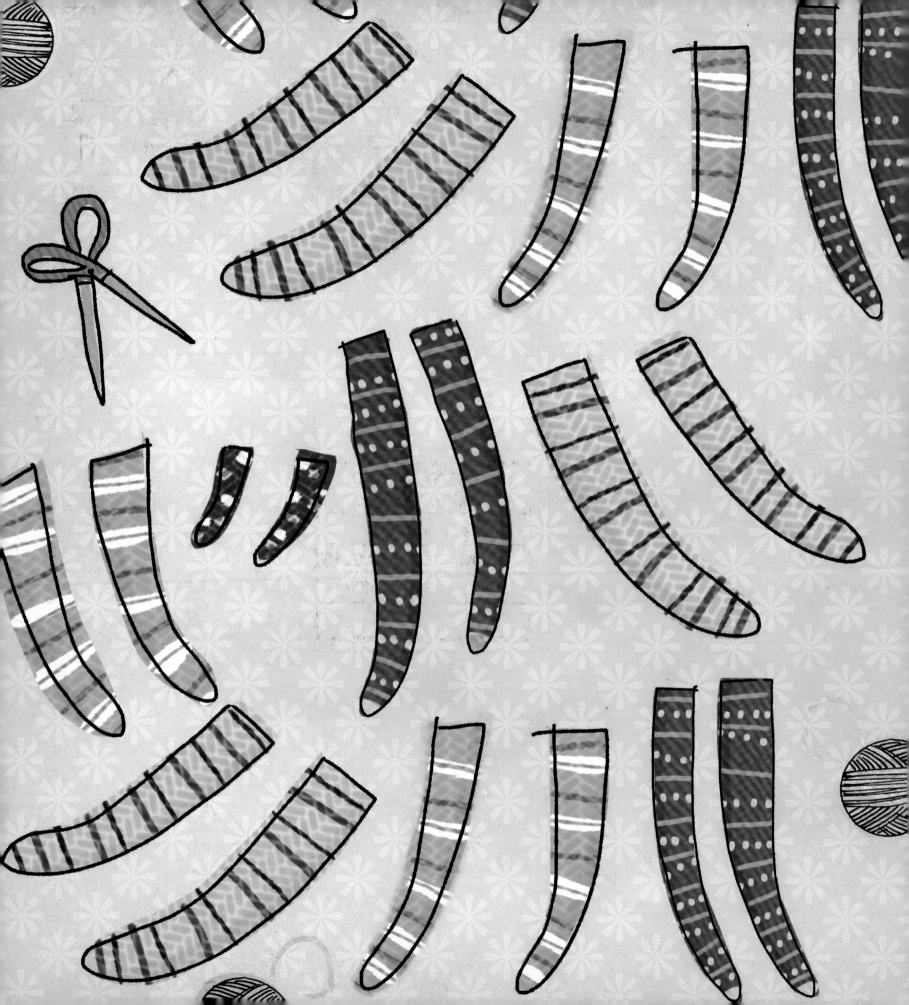

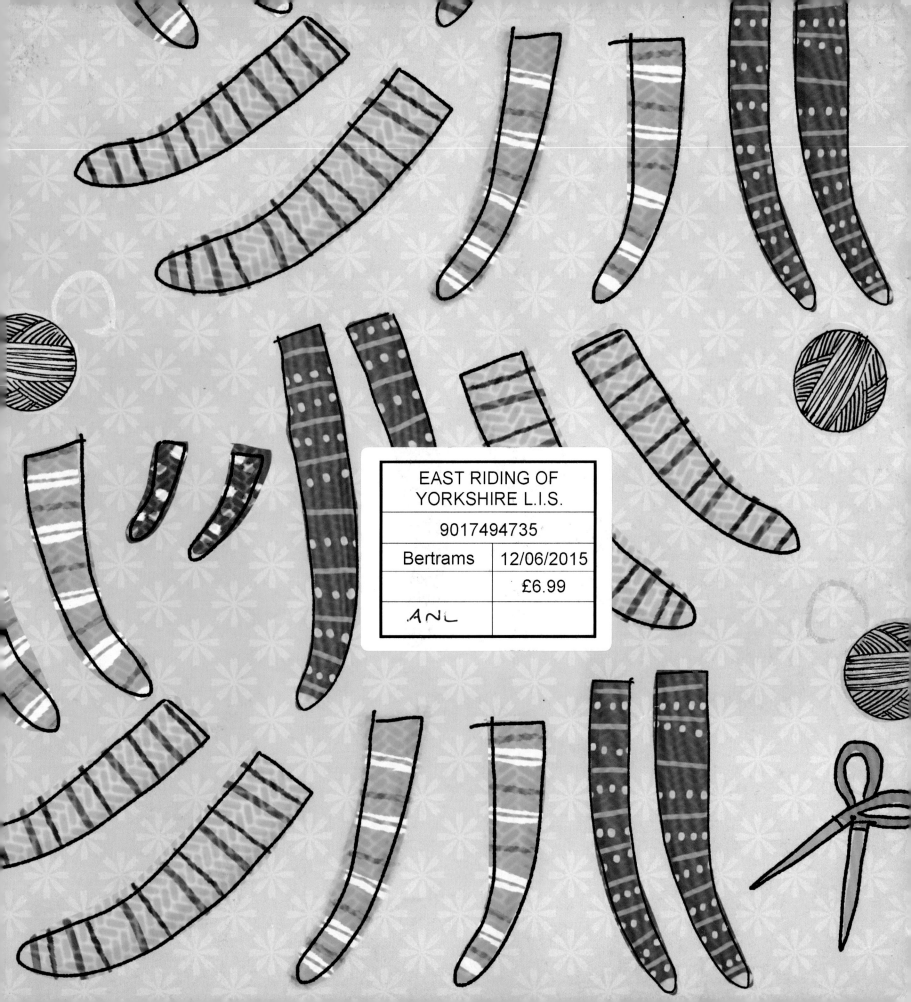

Little Lionel loved to watch Granny Mutton knit. **Clickety-click click** he skipped to the tune of her needles.

Tappity-tap tap, he drummed the box filled with Granny's woollen gifts.

Granny knitted earmuffs
for **big hogs** and...

...jackets for
cool cats and...

...**squishy** cushions
for **squashy** bottoms.

"What's in the box today, Granny? Is it for me?"
Little Lionel asked.

Granny Mutton's teeth clicked in time to her stitches.

"All good things come to those who wait," she said.

But Little Lionel didn't want to wait. "What's in the box? What's in the box?

Can I wear it on my head?

Or cuddle it at night?"

He twirled and whirled until he was dizzy. Granny laughed. "Wear these on your head? No, but they'll keep your friends warm." Granny laid out a row of socks for horse, duck, dog and mouse. Little Lionel counted them.

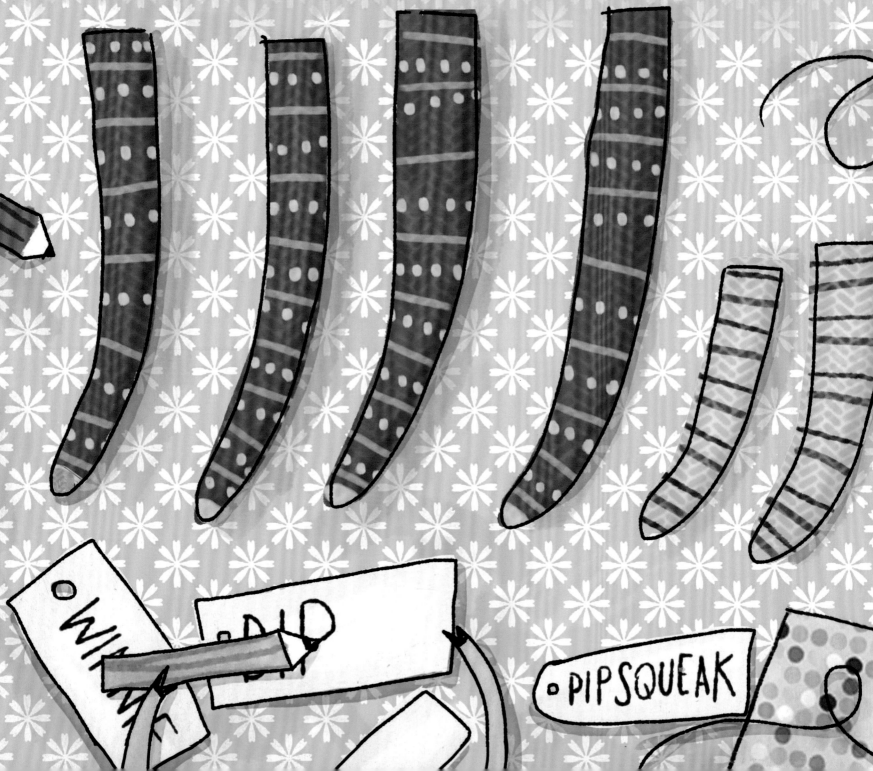

PIPSQUEAK

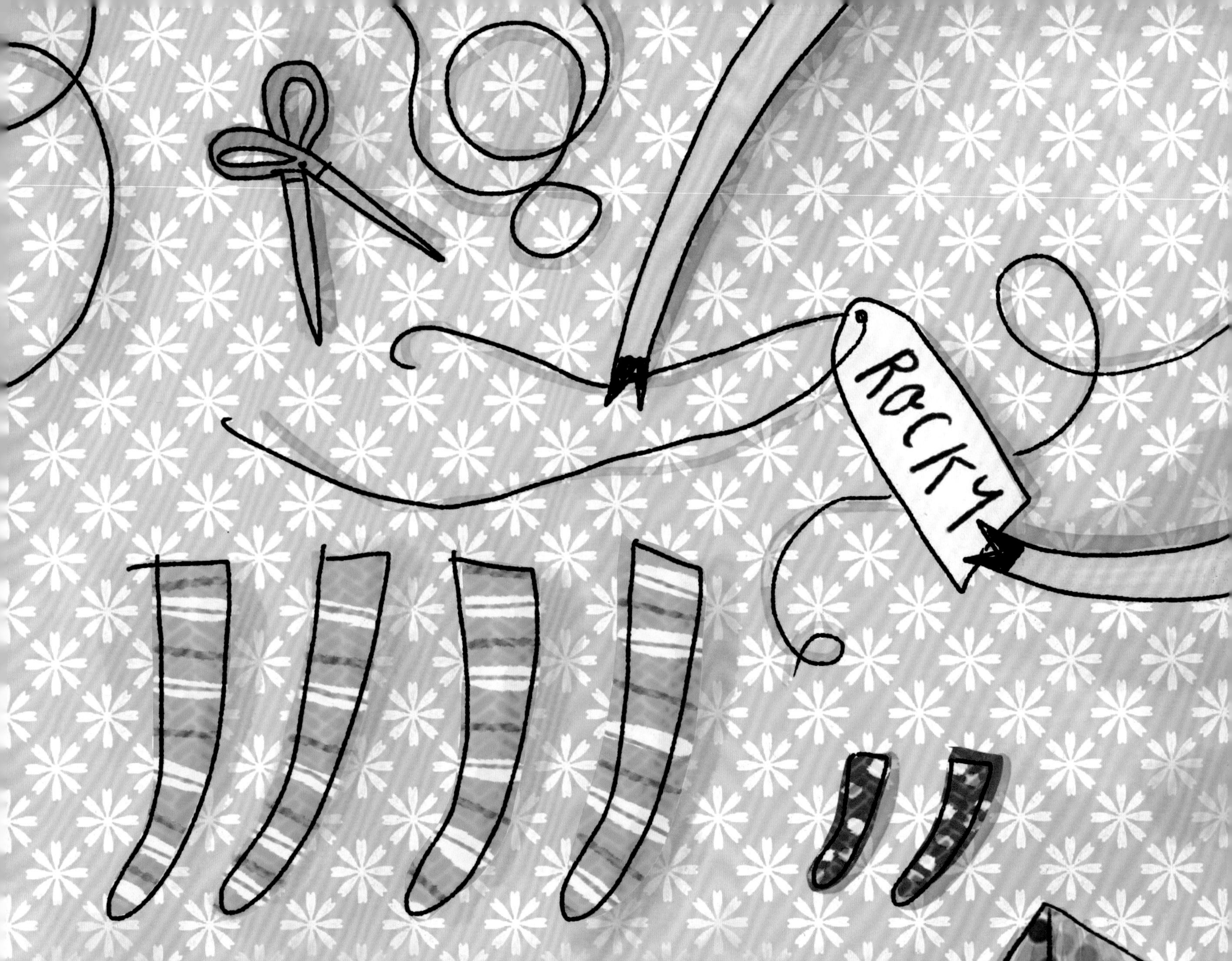

The tag reads: ROCKY

"Top socks, Granny," he said.

He wished he had some too.

He helped tuck labels in the top of
each pair and put them back in the box.

He carried Granny's box past...

the muddy cow field,

Over the rickety stile,

through the wooden gate and into the farmyard.

Rocky the sheep-dog roared by in his cart. Little Lionel jumped. The box soared high. PING! The lid flew open. WHOOSH! Socks and labels scattered across the path.

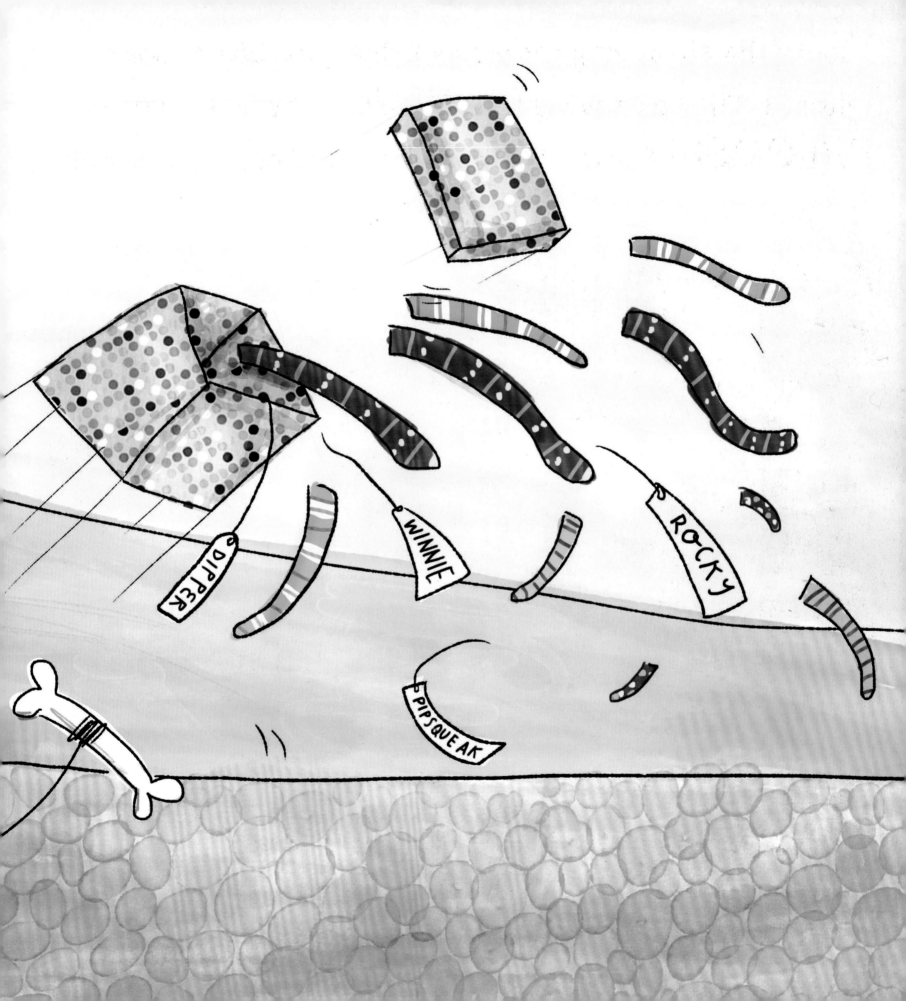

Little Lionel picked them up.

"Look what you've made me do. I can't remember which label belongs to which socks."

He shared out the presents. Winnie squashed and squeezed her big hooves into short spotty socks. "Neigh, these aren't mine."

Pipsqueak tripped and flipped inside a purple stripey sock. "Should socks be as long as tunnels?"

Dipper had too many socks.

ZIG

"Perhaps one is a beak warmer,"
Little Lionel said. "UMMMFFF,"
Dipper shook her head.

Rocky's socks flopped and flapped on his paws. He couldn't steer his cart. He sped across the yard.

ZAG

ZIG

Splat!

He landed in the pig trough.

Whee! Socks flew across the farmyard.

Whizz! One landed in the vegetables.

Pipsqueak found it in the carrots.

He put it on. It was just right.

Rocky flipped a sock at Little Lionel. WHOOSH! He fired one back. Rocky said, "That's the perfect fit."

Socks were tossed and tried
until everyone had the right size.

The animals marched to Granny Mutton's house.

"Top socks, Granny. Everyone looks great," Little Lionel said.

Granny Mutton patted his head. "You helped today, so these are for my number one grandson..."

To his surprise, she popped
sparkly red socks
on his hooves.

Not only were Granny's socks soft
and cosy but they also had that
special feel - socks made with love.

The End

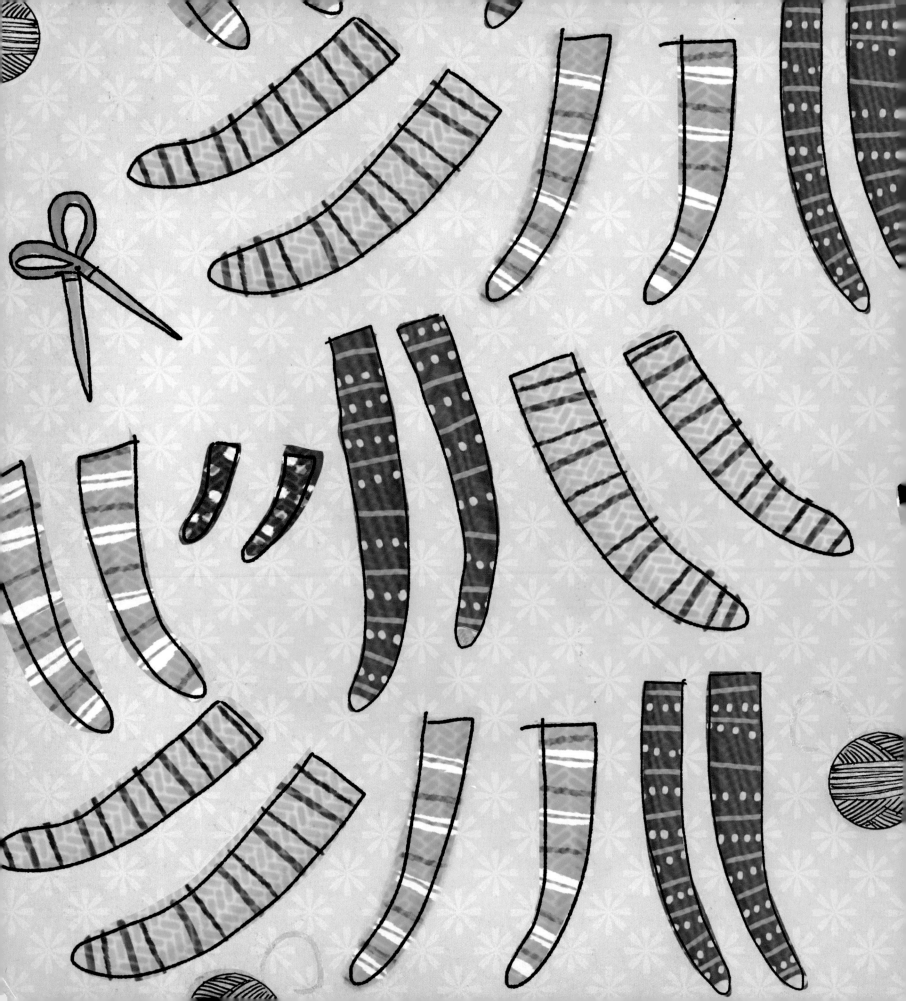

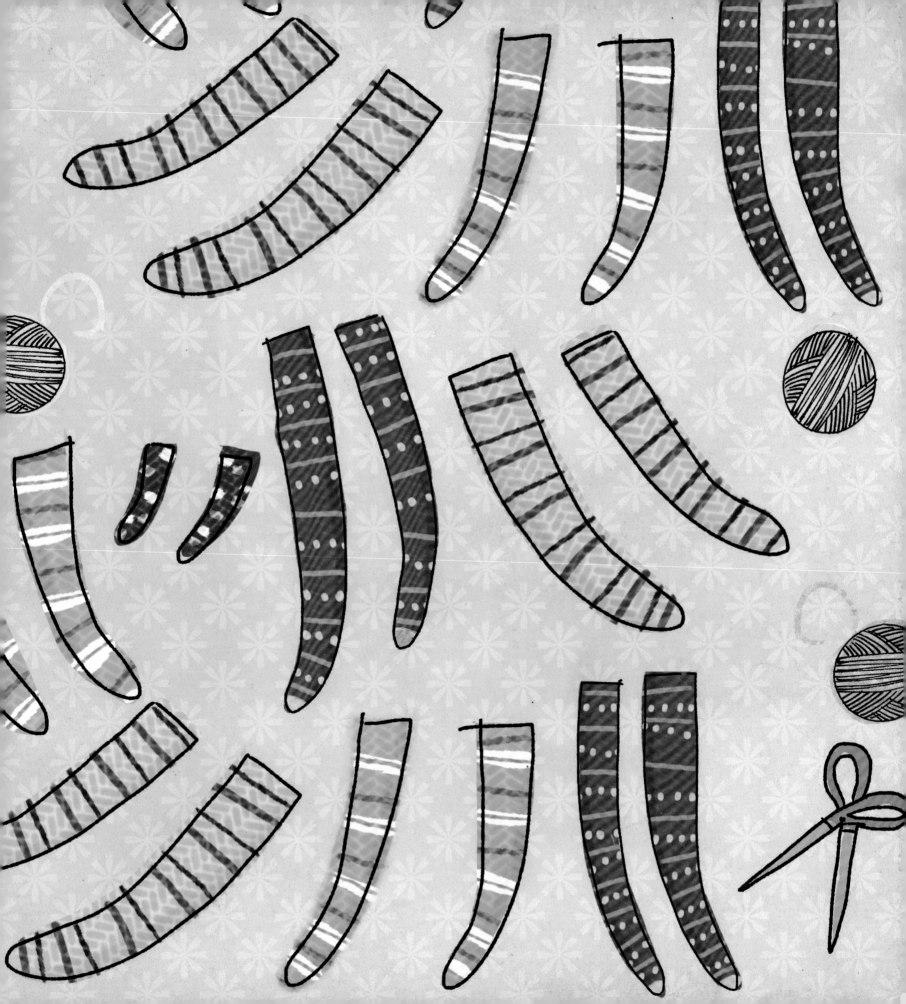

A Box of Socks
is an original concept by © Amanda Brandon

Author: Amanda Brandon

Illustrator: Catalina Echeverri
Catalina is represented by Plum Pudding
www.plumpuddingillustration.com

Published by MAVERICK ARTS PUBLISHING LTD
Studio 3A, City Business Centre, 6 Brighton Road,
Horsham, West Sussex, RH13 5BB, +44 (0)1403 256941
© Maverick Arts Publishing Limited May 2015

ISBN 978-1-84886-170-1

Maverick
arts publishing
www.maverickbooks.co.uk